love you oodles

by – lindsey poluck

For my children-

Always do what you love, and never stop dreaming. With hard work, I know in my heart you can do anything you set your mind to. I love you oodles.

For my family and friends-

Thank you for always supporting me endlessly. I wouldn't be the artist I am today without your love.

Two loving people, in search of a pet,

drove off to the shelter, to see what they could get.

Inside each cage, a bundle of joy.

Awaiting a home, each girl and boy.

Out stretched her paw, gentle and slow.

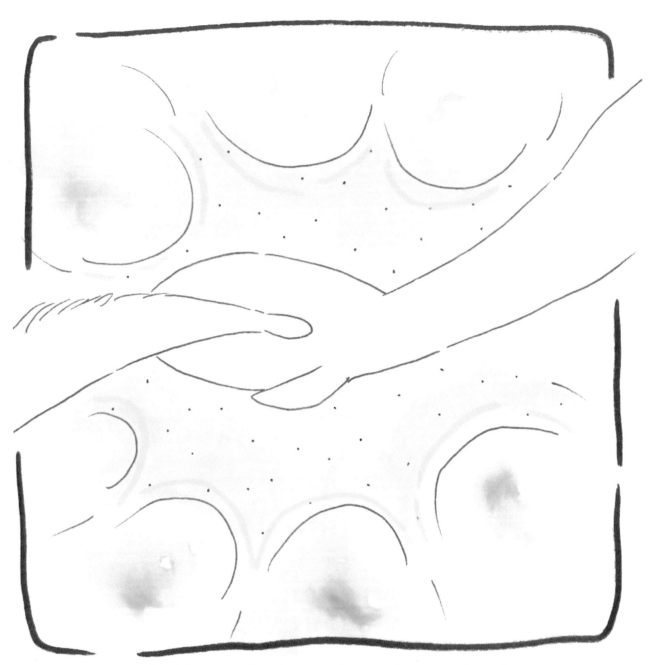

And with one simple touch, set the couple aglow.

They opened the cage, and out jumped the cat.

Right into her dad's arms, she happily sat.

Kitten in tow, they went to the store.

Then hurried back home, so she could explore.

With each jump and bounce it was blatantly clear,

that this little kitten was meant to be here.

"What is her name?" the young couple blundered.

"Salli or Sophie or Mika?" they wondered.

Nothing quite fit but they loved her oodles.

Then it just clicked, "We'll call her Doodle!"

Doodle

About the Author

Lindsey is a stay-at-home mother and passionate cartoon artist. She spends her time trying to not only inspire her children to create and explore, but to create something new herself everyday. She strives to make artwork and stories that would bring a smile to anyone's face.

Thank you for supporting a small-time artist and author. I hope this book brings you and your family many smiles for years to come.

Made in the USA
Middletown, DE
20 October 2022

13042826R00015